Shoo Rayner

ROMAN BRIT

BOAR WARS

ORCHARD BOOKS
338 Euston Road, London NW1 3BH
Orchard Books Australia
Level 17/207 Kent Street, Sydney, NSW 2000

First published in 2015 by Orchard Books
This paperback edition published in 2015
ISBN 978 1 40833 455 3

A CIP catalogue record for this book is available
from the British Library.

1 3 5 7 9 10 8 6 4 2

Printed and bound by CPI Group (UK) Ltd, Croydon, CR0 4YY

Orchard Books is an imprint of Hachette Children's Group
and published by The Watts Publishing Group Limited, an Hachette UK company.

www.hachette.co.uk

Shoo Rayner

ROMAN BRIT

BOAR WARS

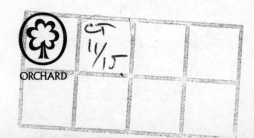

ORCHARD

FORT FINIS TERRAE is a sleepy backwater in the great Roman Empire. A young shepherd boy named Brit lives there with his sheep and faithful dog Festus.

It's a quiet life for Brit and his animals in the fort. But every so often, something happens to make it a day to remember!

GERMANIA

ARABIA

CHAPTER ONE

"What would happen if the barbarians attacked us now?" Brit wondered aloud, as he dumped his heavy sheaf of barley on the hay cart.

"Ha!" laughed Bumptius Matius, the Chief Engineer. "There haven't been barbarians round here for as long as I can remember."

Brit stood up to stretch his aching back and looked all around him. The sun was beating down on the soldiers of the legion, who were all in their underpants, cutting and tying stacks of barley.

The soldiers had very little to do these days. They just helped out wherever they were needed. Right now, the barley needed to be harvested for the winter, and everyone was pitching in.

"There's no need to worry about barbarians!" bellowed a loud voice behind them. The soldiers stood to attention as Gluteus Maximus, the Fort Commander, came striding across the field towards them.

"Barbarians!" squeaked the girl at his side. "There aren't any barbarians here, are there Daddy?"

Gluteus Maximus smiled at his daughter and spoke in a gentle voice. "There are no barbarians, my little sweetie pie. Just this field of barley to get safely cut and stored away."

He turned back to the soldiers and bellowed, "What are you waiting for you lazy oafs? Get back to work! That barley won't stack itself!"

"Err… it's not just the barley, sir,"
said Bumptius Matius, bowing his head
and saluting. "There's the apples in the
orchard too. They'll be ripe for picking any
moment. Someone needs to go down there
and keep the birds away."

"Festus and I can do that!" Brit said
chirpily. "Festus loves chasing birds,"
he added, smiling at his beloved dog.

Anything was better than carrying these heavy stacks of barley around.

"And I can help, can't I, Daddy?" Drusilla fluttered her eyelashes. The Fort Commander's stern expression melted away instantly.

"Of course you can my little Drusi-woo," he said lovingly. "Though no little birds could be scared of you!"

Oh, great! Brit thought. *That's just what I need!*

Drusilla wasn't exactly Brit's boss, but he still had to listen to her. As the Fort Commander's daughter, she was sort of in charge, and she had sort of taken him under her wing. There was nothing he could do about it. He was stuck with her!

"Mind you keep the gate shut!"
Bumptius Matius called after them. "Don't
let the wild boar in. They can eat all the
apples in the orchard in an afternoon,
especially that big one…Gargantua!"

"Wild boar! Gargantua!" Drusilla's voice
trembled with excitement and fear. "You
will protect me, won't you, Brit?"

Brit rolled his eyes. This was going to be
a long afternoon!

CHAPTER TWO

"Leave the chickens alone!" Brit yelled, as Festus bounced into the orchard. The chickens squawked and ran in all directions.

"And stay away from the beehives!" Brit added. "Do you want to get stung all over?"

Festus tucked his tail between his legs and bounded back.

"What do we do now?" asked Drusilla.

Brit turned his face to the warm sun, closed his eyes and smiled. "Nothing," he said.

"Nothing?" Drusilla, sounded disappointed.

"Nothing," Brit said again dreamily. "My back is aching from carrying sheaves of barley all day. I'm going to have a quiet afternoon testing to see if the apples are ripe. Festus can keep the birds away all on his own, can't you, boy?"

Festus panted in reply. His tongue lolled and spit dribbled from the side of his mouth.

Brit reached up to a nearby tree to pick an apple – and caught sight of something alarming.

"Oh!" he said, and stepped back a couple of paces.

"What is it?" Drusilla asked.

"Look!" Brit crouched down behind the tree. "Just up there."

Cautiously, Drusilla stepped closer. She screwed up her eyes and followed Brit's gaze.

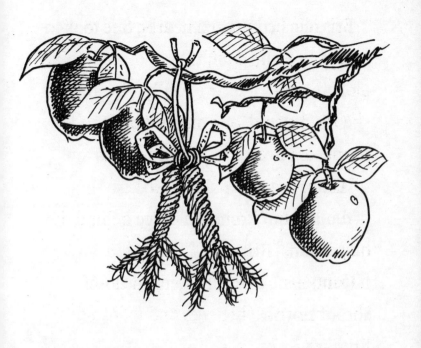

A bunch of barley stalks were braided together. They were hanging from a branch in the tree.

"What is it?" Drusilla asked again.

Brit looked around warily and whispered as quietly as he could. "I think it might be…Druids!"

Drusilla's eyes opened wide. She took in a deep breath.

"B-b-but Druids are b-b-barbarians," she stammered. "I-i-if there are Druids, then there must be b-b-barbarians too!"

"I suppose that anyone who isn't actually from Rome was once a barbarian," Brit said. "The barbarians haven't gone away, they just became sort of British Romans."

He reached up and picked two shiny, red apples. He polished one on his tunic and offered it to Drusilla.

"Are we allowed to eat them?" Drusilla asked. "Won't the Druids mind?"

Brit sunk his teeth into the juicy flesh of his apple. "It's okay, we're just testing them to see if they're ripe."

"Mmmmm! They're so sweet!" Apple juice trickled down Drusilla's chin.

"Delicious!" Brit smiled. "They're definitely ripe. We should let Bumptious Matius know they're ready for picking."

Festus growled and stared at the gate.

"What's the matter with him?" Drusilla asked.

"He just wants some apple!" Brit laughed and offered Festus his apple core. But Festus ignored it and continued growling.

"Listen!" there was a hint of fear in Drusilla's voice. "Can you hear it? It's the Druids! I knew we shouldn't have eaten their apples!"

Brit cocked his ear and listened intently.

Yes…there was a noise…a low, deep, snuffling and grunting sort of noise. There was only one thing that made a snuffling and a grunting noise and it wasn't a Druid… it was a WILD BOAR!

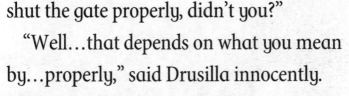

Brit turned to Drusilla. "You did shut the gate properly, didn't you?"

"Well…that depends on what you mean by…properly," said Drusilla innocently. Brit groaned. Typical Drusilla!

CHAPTER THREE

Being careful not to make any noise, Brit and Festus ran quickly towards the gate. The rope on the gate was hanging loose. As the last one through, Drusilla should have looped it around the gatepost.

The snuffling and grunting sounds were coming even closer. Keeping very low, Brit picked up the rope and tried to flick it over the gatepost. He missed. He tried again, and again, and again.

Suddenly, Brit sensed that he was being watched. Slowly he looked up and found himself staring through the bars of the gate – into the small, piggy eyes of an enormous boar!

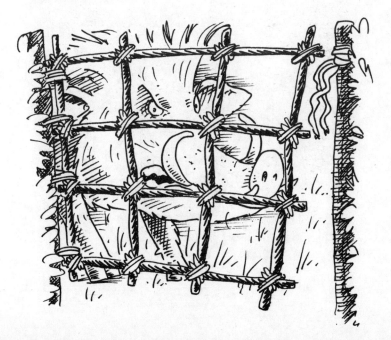

Festus barked and ran at the gate.

"It's Gargantua!" Brit yelled. "Quick! Drusilla! Climb that tree as fast as you can!"

As he ran for his life, Brit heard grunting and barking behind him. Festus couldn't hold off a beast like that forever.

Brit swung himself up into the branches of the tree. "Come on, Drusilla!"

Drusilla was rooted to the spot, frozen with panic and fear.

"Quick! Hold my hand!" Brit yelled.

The gate slammed open, knocking Festus out of the way. Gargantua stormed into the orchard, snuffling and snorting and looking for trouble.

Drusilla screamed. Gargantua growled, lowered his head and charged.

Festus barked like a maniac. The chickens squawked and ran for safety. Drusilla screamed again. Brit grabbed her hands and pulled her out of harm's way, just as Gargantua crashed into the tree.

The tree shuddered. The roots rocked.

The trunk swayed and… thud, thud thud… apples fell on the grass below.

"Thunk!" One large apple fell heavily on Gargantua's head. He stopped and looked around suspiciously,  wondering where it had come from.

Festus stopped barking. The children held their breath.

Gargantua spotted the apple. He lowered his head and snaffled it up in one swift crunch!

With a grunt of appreciation, he ate another apple, then another and another.

Quite forgetting Festus and the children, Gargantua raised his head and hollered with a loud, squealing, cry.

"What's he doing?" Drusilla whimpered.

Brit bit his lip. "I think – I think he might be calling his friends."

Sure enough, the children soon heard the sound of trotters drumming on the soft ground. There must be at least thirty of them, thought Brit. One by one, an enormous herd of boars entered the orchard.

Brit and Drusilla watched in fear as Gargantua showed the other boars how to bump into tree trunks to make the apples fall. In what seemed like no time at all, the orchard was filled with the sound of apples thudding on the ground and the boars snuffling and crunching.

"They're going to eat up all the apples!" said Brit. "We've got to do something."

"But Brit!" Drusilla said fearfully. "Gargantua will eat you!"

"I think he's more interested in the apples," said Brit in a brave voice, carefully swinging down from the tree.

"Don't leave me!" Drusilla whimpered.

"You'll be fine," Brit assured her. "Just stay where you are." He gave her a stern look. "Don't move!"

CHAPTER FOUR

Brit crawled towards the gate on his hands and knees, using the long grass as cover. Festus, thinking it was a game, danced all around him, drawing attention to where he was.

"Festus," Brit hissed. "You daft thing! Get down!" Festus lay down and licked Brit's face, with his long, hot, dribbly tongue.

Finally, Brit made it to the gate. He jumped up and ran, faster than he ever had before, across the meadow and into the wide-open field.

The soldiers, still wearily chopping barley, all stopped and stared at him in surprise.

"It's Gargantua!" Brit yelled at them. "He's in the orchard!"

The soldiers sprang to attention immediately. Finally, something exciting for them to do! They rallied, ready for action…even if they were in their underpants!

"Where's Drusilla?" boomed Gluteus Maximus, his loud voice tinted with fear.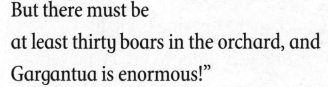

"She's safe," said Brit. "She's hiding up a tree. But there must be at least thirty boars in the orchard, and Gargantua is enormous!"

The Fort Commander drew himself up to his full height and roared orders at his men. "You!" he cried, pointing at the largest group of soldiers. "Go and surround the orchard now. There may be more boars on the way."

"You!" he pointed at a smaller group.
"Go back to the fort and bring the
Scorpion. We're going to need a powerful
weapon to vanquish this enemy! Let's go!"

The soldiers cheered. The *Scorpion* was
the legion's giant crossbow. The men had
a proper job to do at last! Together, they
stormed across the field, waving their
scythes and sickles in the air.

Soon the orchard was surrounded. The Fort Commander stood by the gate and looked for Drusilla.

"Are you all right, my little apple dumpling?" he called.

"No!" Drusilla's voice squeaked from the leafy branches. "I'm stuck up a tree, hiding from boars!"

Brit rolled his eyes again. Even in grave danger, Drusilla was still being Drusilla!

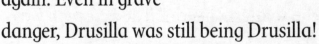

"Just stay where you are, poppet, and keep very still," Gluteus Maximus called back, clearly trying to stay calm. "The artillery will be here any moment."

Soon enough, Brit could hear the chants and shouts of the *Scorpion* crew, as they hauled their deadly weapon along the chalky lane from the fort.

"Right, men," ordered the Commander. "Get yourselves set up here. That's Gargantua there – you can't miss him. He's enormous!"

The Scorpion
creaked and
groaned as one
of the soldiers
wound back its
arms.

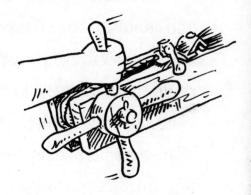

"Load the
bolt!"

A soldier inserted a long, feathered bolt.

"Take aim!"

"He's staggering about a lot, Sir!" said the soldier, pointing at Gargantua. "Anyone would think he was drunk!"

"Fire!" ordered the commander.

The *Scorpion's* bow snapped tight. The bolt whistled across the orchard, straight and true.

Just as the bolt flew towards him,
Gargantua's legs gave way. He toppled
to the floor, and the bolt zipped through
the thick bristles on his head, giving him
a very stylish parting.

"Reload!" ordered the commander.

Gargantua had eaten so many apples that he couldn't stand up straight! After what looked like a great amount of effort, the boar finally managed to stagger to his feet, though he looked very wobbly – like a grumpy old man who has had too much beer in the tavern.

"Take aim!" ordered the commander again.

"He keeps moving, sir!" complained the soldiers.

"Fire!"

"No! Not there!" yelled Brit, but it was too late.

The bolt sang out across the orchard, whisking past Gargantua's ears, and landing fair and square – a perfect shot – in the middle of a beehive, knocking it off the little platform that it stood on.

Within seconds, the sky turned as dark as a storm. A cloud of angry, buzzing bees filled the air. Drusilla let out a shriek of terror from her tree.

Brit looked on in horror as the bees swarmed around the orchard. But then he noticed something.

"Look!" he called. "The bees are all heading towards Gargantua."

It was as if the bees had decided that the big hairy thing in the orchard was responsible for the destruction of their home – and he was going to pay for it.

All at once, as if they were one giant bee, the swarm poured down on Gargantua, attacking his enormous, hairy bottom.

The giant boar's squealing screams echoed round the countryside, leaving a moment of shocked silence in their wake.

The other boars panicked and started squealing. The swarm of bees turned in formation and began attacking them, too!

The orchard was in a state of pandemonium. Brit put his fingers in his ears as he watched the wobbly animals

run madly in all directions. They crashed
through the fence, where a group of
soldiers were standing guard. Their earlier
excitement forgotten, the men screamed
and ran away as fast as they could.

The bees didn't like soldiers either.
They swarmed after them, over the hill
and out of sight.

CHAPTER FIVE

For a long while, Brit stayed exactly where he was, ducked down in the long grass by the orchard fence. He couldn't leave Drusilla on her own. The bees were gone – but Gargantua was still in there.

Festus lay next to him, still and quiet as a mouse. He wasn't afraid of Gargantua, but he was afraid of bees.

The great boar was still tottering
around the orchard on his little piggy feet,
squealing at the pain of the bee stings,
rubbing his bottom against the tree trunks
and falling over every now and then.

"Psst!" Brit hissed. "Drusilla? Are
you okay?"

"No!" Drusilla's voice rang out. "I am STILL stuck up a tree!"

"Keep still," said Brit. "I'll come and get you in a minute."

With a heavy thump, Gargantua collapsed on the ground again. His eyelids drooped and fluttered. Soon enough, he was grunting and snoring in a deep, apple-fuelled sleep.

Brit untied the rope from the gate and made a loop at one end. He carefully placed the loop over Gargantua's huge tusky mouth and pulled it tight.

Gargantua opened one eye slowly. Brit froze. A single bloodshot eyeball stared at him blankly. The boar huffed and went back to sleep again.

Quickly, with the rest of the rope, Brit tied the giant animal's legs together. *When he wakes up again,* Brit thought, *he's going nowhere!*

Festus sniffed Gargantua's ears. The giant beast grunted in his groggy, appley dreams.

"It's okay," Brit called to Drusilla up in the tree. "You can come down now."

"I can't!" Drusilla shouted. Her voice was a little shakier than normal. "I'm stuck!"

Brit climbed up the tree and helped her back down, branch by branch.

"Finally," she barked at him, when she had reached the ground. "I thought you were going to leave me up there forever!"

She was trying to look brave, but Brit could see she'd been scared. She was as white as a sheet, her hands were trembling and her knees were shaking.

Brit led Drusilla to the tumbled-over beehive. He scooped out a piece of honeycomb and handed it to her. "Here, eat some of this."

The sweet, sticky honey soon restored Drusilla to her old self. She stood upright and beamed at Brit.

"I suppose we'd better go and tell
everyone how we captured Gargantua!"
she said cheerily. "Daddy will be so
pleased with us."

Brit opened his mouth to correct
her. Surely it was he who had done the
capturing! But Drusilla was Drusilla. She
had a way of changing things round to her

way of thinking. What was the point?

Brit whistled to Festus. "Come on, boy. Let's go and find the army."

CHAPTER SIX

Two days later and the harvest
was finished. The field had been cut.
The barley had been separated, the
barleycorns stored and the stalks built
into haystacks.

The apples – the ones that the boars hadn't eaten – had been picked and carefully stored away for the winter.

Gluteus Maximus was delighted, and proclaimed the harvest a great success. He ordered a celebration supper to be served in the courtyard of Fort Finnis Terrae.

All day long, delicious smells of freshly baked barley bread, honey cakes and blackberry-and-apple pie floated on the air. But there was one smell, above all others, that had everybody's mouth watering.

"A harvest toast!" called Drusilla's dad, at the supper that evening. "To my darling daughter Drusilla, the Queen of the Harvest, who captured Gargantua all on her own!"

The crowd raised their cups. "To Drusilla!"

Drusilla, decked in fresh flowers and
a crown of braided barley stalks, looked
shyly at the ground and shrugged her
shoulders as if to say, "it was nothing".

Brit shook his head. How had she
claimed all the glory? She had told the
story so well of how she had tied up the
boar, he almost believed it himself!

"And here's to the beast," Drusilla's dad raised his cup towards the fire.

"The founder of this delicious meal!"

Suspended above a mound of glowing, red-hot charcoal, an enormous boar turned slowly, round and round on a spit.

A huge red apple was planted firmly in its tusks. Delicious aromas of roast pork filled the air.

The crowd rose to their feet, held their drinking vessels high in the air and called with one voice.

"To Gargantua!"

ROMAN BRIT

COLLECT THEM ALL!